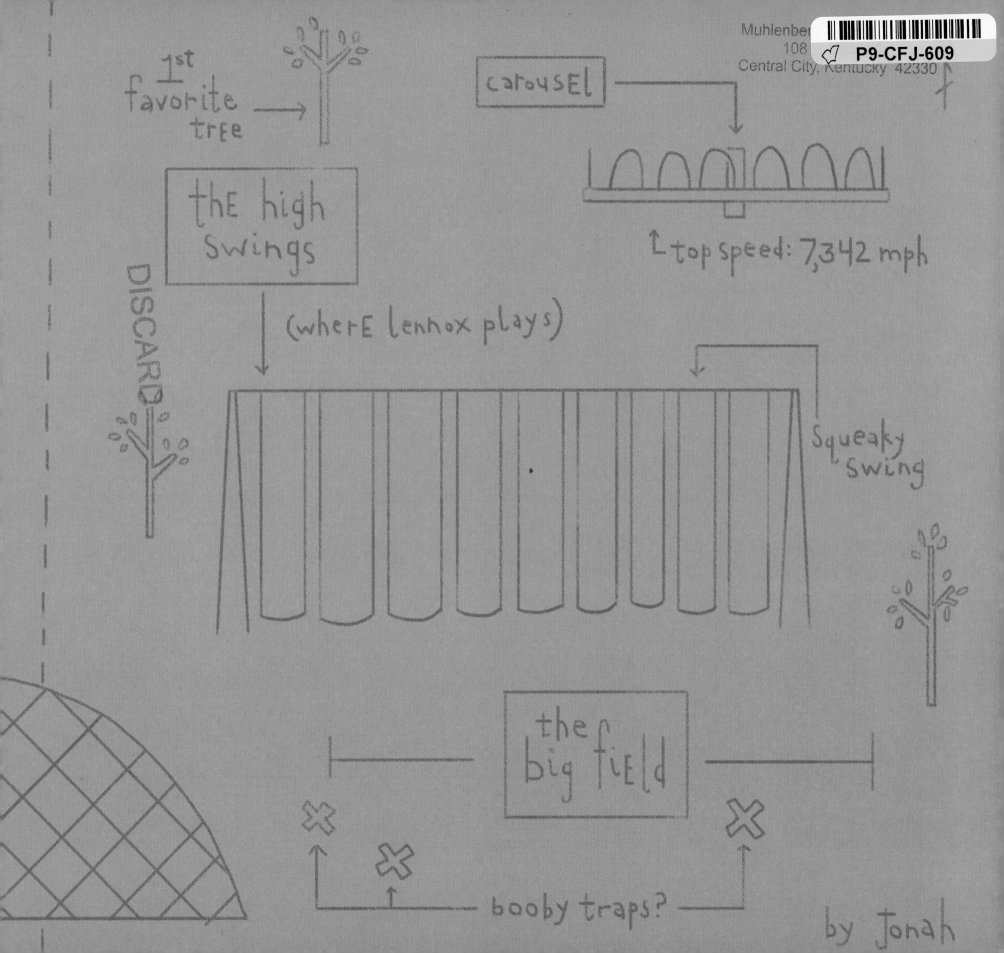

1st favorite tree →

carousel →

↳ top speed: 7,342 mph

the high swings

DISCARD

↓ (where lennox plays)

Squeaky Swing

the big field

booby traps?

by Jonah

*To Nikki*
*for building me a kingdom*
*and filling it with rulers*

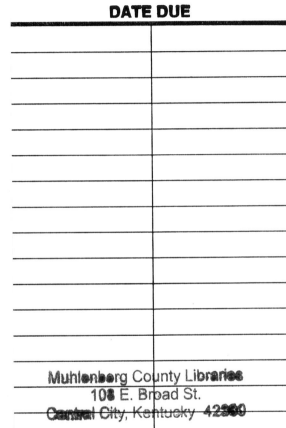

# rulers of the
# playground

## Joseph Kuefler

BALZER + BRAY
*An Imprint of HarperCollins Publishers*

One morning, Jonah decided to become ruler of the playground.

"I am now king of this land," announced Jonah.
"Promise to obey me and I'll let you play
in my kingdom."

Jonah's kingdom had slides,
so everyone pinkie promised.

And just like that, Jonah became
king of the playground.

And generous . . .
"Who's hungry?"

. . . most of the time.
"You can share this cracker."

Everyone played in King Jonah's kingdom.

Everyone except for Lennox . . .

because she wanted to rule the playground, too.

"This side of the playground is now mine," announced Lennox. "Cross your heart and promise to follow my rules."

Lennox's kingdom had swings,
so they crossed their hearts and promised.

And just like that, Lennox became
a mighty queen.

Queen Lennox was wise . . .

"Watch this!"

. . . in most cases.
"I totally meant to do that."

And patient . . .
"Take your time."

. . . most days.
"OKAY, ENOUGH ALREADY!"

Everyone played in Queen Lennox's kingdom.

Everyone except for King Jonah.

"This playground is mine!" hollered King Jonah.

"Is not!" shouted Queen Lennox. "It's all mine!"

And just like that, the playground was divided in two.

King Jonah and Queen Lennox each made a plan to grow their kingdoms.

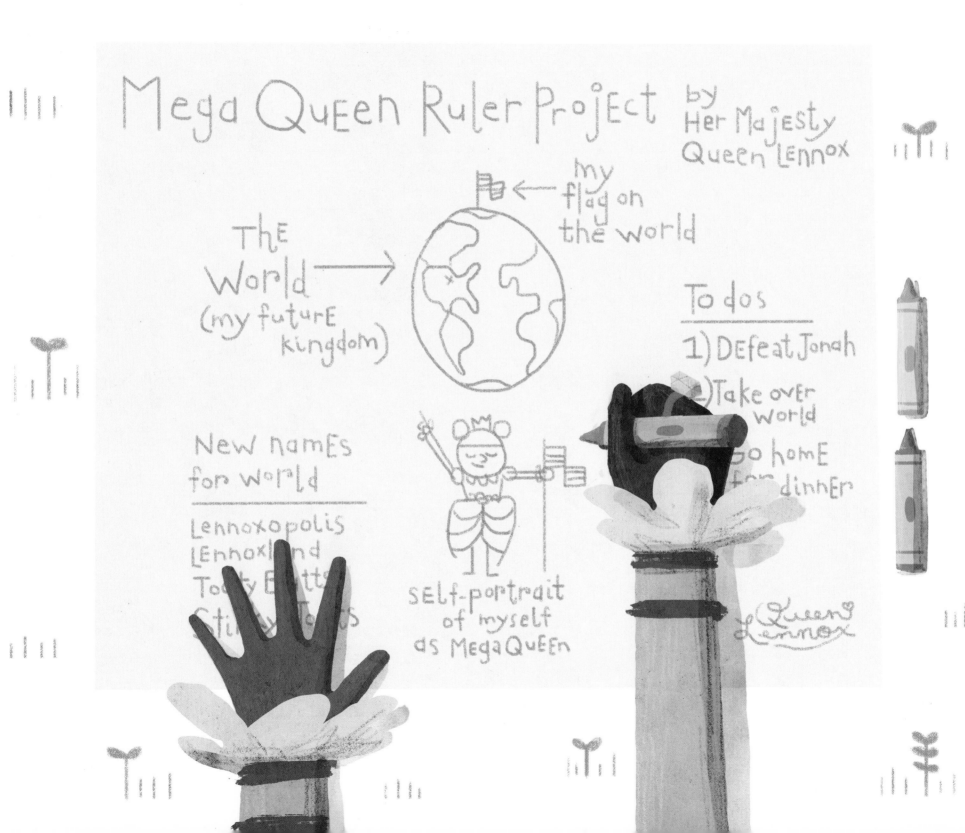

They conquered small things . . .

"Push!" said King Jonah.
"HARDER!"

"Spin!" said Queen Lennox.
"Faster! FASTER!"

and big things . . .

"CLIMB!" shouted King Jonah.

"HIGHER!" hollered Queen Lennox.

They even tried to conquer Augustine's dog,
Sir Hamilton Humphrey Hildebrand III.

"STAY!" hollered
King Jonah.

"FETCH!" shouted
Queen Lennox.

King Jonah and Queen Lennox claimed the entire playground.

Until there was nothing left to conquer . . .

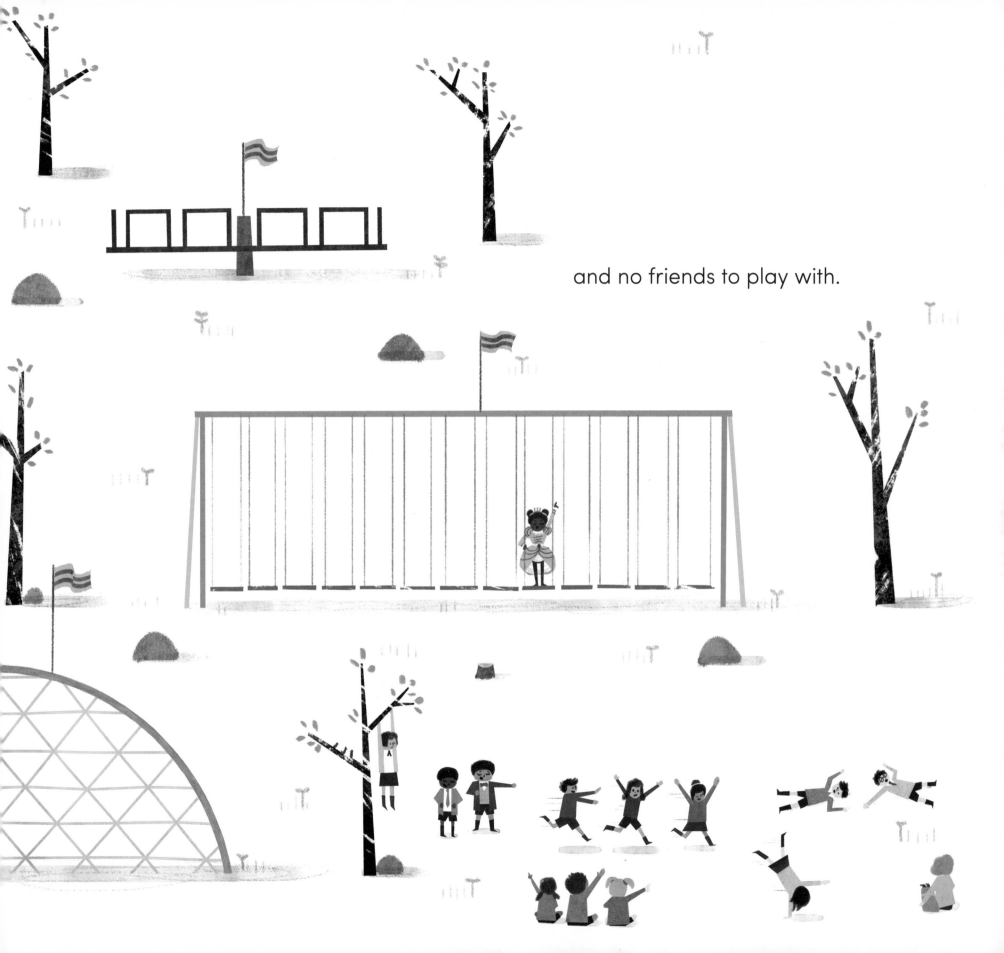

and no friends to play with.

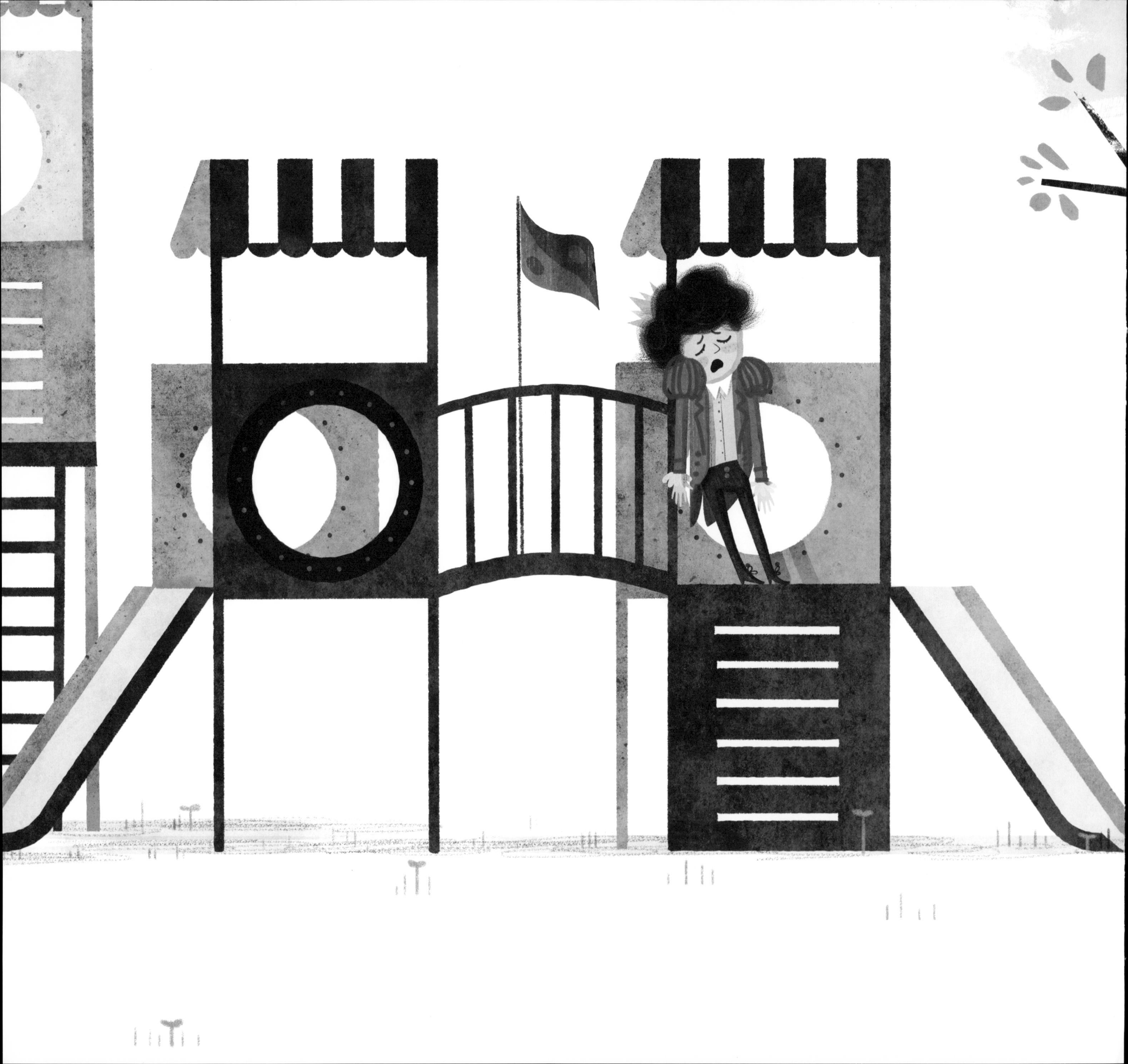

"Conquering is complicated,"
said King Jonah.

"Yeah," said Queen Lennox.
"Super complicated."

So they made a new plan.

They took down their royal flags.
They gave back their kingdoms.

Jonah stopped being king.

Lennox stopped being queen.

"We're done conquering," said Jonah.

"We cross our hearts and promise
to never be rulers again," said Lennox.

And just like that, the playground was fun again.

Everyone was happy . . .

except for Augustine . . .

and Sir Hamilton Humphrey Hildebrand III.

Balzer + Bray is an imprint of HarperCollins Publishers.

Rulers of the Playground

ISBN 978-0-06-242432-7

Typography by Joseph Kuefler and Dana Fritts
16 17 18 19 20 SCP 10 9 8 7 6 5 4 3 2 1

First Edition

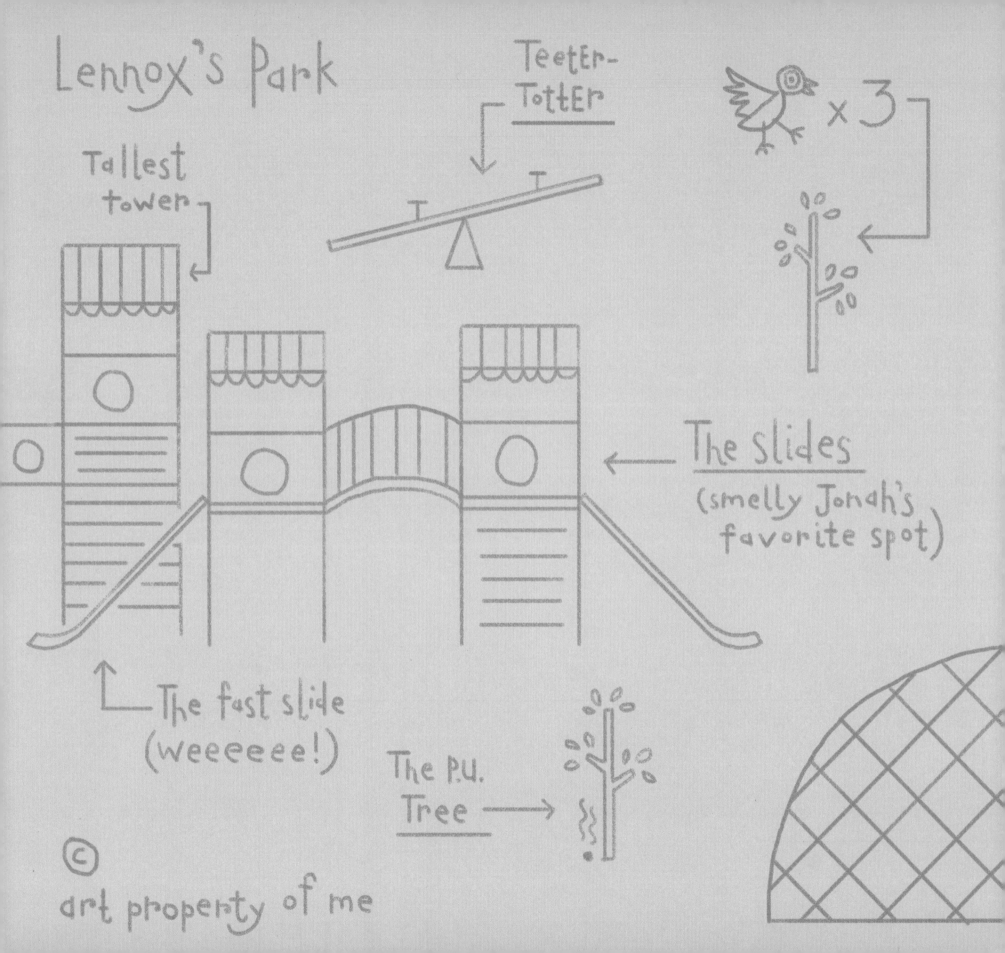